Donk Magical Gift

Trella Dudley Wallis

Copyright © 2024 *Trella Dudley-Wallis*

All rights reserved. No part of this publication may be reproduced, distributed, or transmitted in any form or by any means without the prior written permission of the author.

ISBN: 979-8-303948-50-1

Piccolo Patterson Publishing

DEDICATION

I dedicate this book to all those working tirelessly around the world to help donkeys, mules and horses in need. Treating them kindly in the face of unkindness, bringing the care and compassion that all life deserves and making our shared world a better place for them to live in.

Profits from this book will be donated to a range of animal charities operating in many countries around the world, supporting donkey welfare.

ACKNOWLEDGMENTS

I would like to acknowledge Latifa Oubennacer whose vivid illustrations have helped to bring Donkey's story to life. Living in Morocco, she has seen first-hand the vital work of international animal welfare charities helping working donkeys in day-to-day life, as well as in the suffering of natural disaster, alongside people.

I would also like to acknowledge Kevin and my other proof readers for their time and patience in proofreading my stories, which oddly seem to grow in length each time. The magic never ends!

ABOUT THE AUTHOR

Whilst organising a Halloween fundraising Event at her local Donkey Sanctuary, the author felt that a focal point was needed for completion. So, with a myth and magic theme in mind, the story of 'Donkey's Magical Gift' came into being ! With initial sponsorship from a toothpaste company, a limited number of bespoke versions of the story were created. This has already supported the work of specific donkey rescue charities around the UK and been enjoyed by readers of all ages. Another Halloween story then quickly followed, as the author works on a series of animal themed stories. These will support the vital work of various animal rescue charities around the country and indeed world. With a keen interest in animals since a young age and so many stories waiting to be told, the author still has so much more to do. With time and imagination, the author hopes to extend her range of stories even further. In recent years, the author has raised thousands of pounds from her voluntary charitable efforts and hopes to continue in her mission to raise vital funds. This will provide on-going support to the amazing charity work already being done. All fundraising and writing is undertaken in a voluntary capacity, to help as many animals in need as possible. The author is also developing other creative ideas of a different genre. She hopes to bring it to fruition very soon.

One day, the three witches wanted to go shopping in town. They were being shown the way by Donkey from the Animal Sanctuary.

The witches did not know it, but they were fast approaching the black hole without stairs. They did not see it because they were arguing about who had the worst teeth. Luckily, Donkey had noticed the danger.

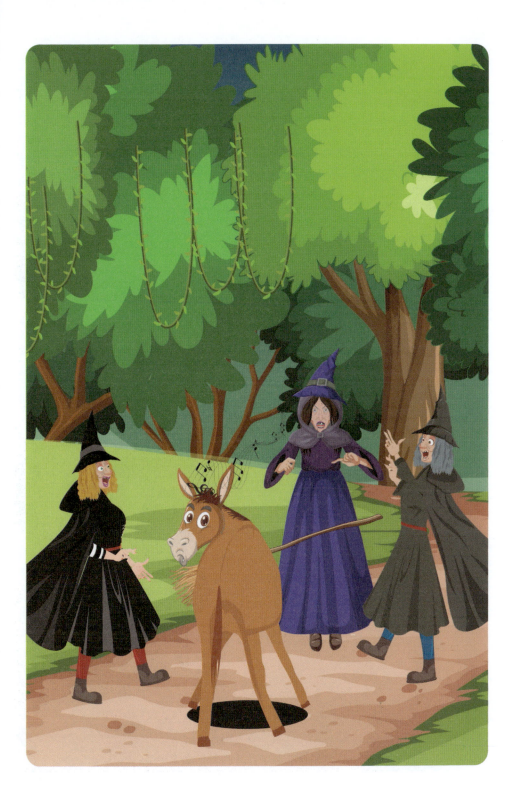

As they approached, Donkey let out a long-winded musical bray and blocked their path to shield them from the black hole.

The witches stopped in their tracks and immediately fell silent. Looking up, they could see that Donkey had saved them from falling into the bottomless black hole without stairs; a fate worse than endless wind from rancid toad stew.

The witches broke into rapturous applause as they chortled and cackled, bearing blackened teeth as they grimaced at Donkey in gratitude. 'I am sure we would have seen that!' said one of the witches proudly, who suddenly stopped clapping and played it down.

Nonetheless, Donkey had been the one to save them for another day of grim tales and trickery. Not even the 'dire need' spell issued by the Oracle could have saved them from this situation. (Witches keep it sewn into the lining of their pocket for use in an emergency).

'We shall reward you for your foresight and bravery,' said another of the witches, waving their wand about.

'I don't need rewards,' replied Donkey in surprise. I helped you because I could,' he continued, 'using the skills, talents and abilities I possess.'
'Just care and kindness is all I need.'

Having said that..' Donkey stopped to think for a moment with his eyes rolling into the ether, as he considered all prospects. 'A juicy carrot would actually be very welcome right about now, or a mint sweet...or two. In fact, three would be just perfect.'

The witches each conjured up a treat for Donkey. He munched and swallowed them immediately, after which, he beamed a cheerful smile. Donkey has good teeth. He brushes twice a day.

'But you should have something really special,' said the third witch. 'Afterall, in saving us, we can go on casting unpleasant spells for all eternity.' 'What did you have in mind?' asked Donkey enquiringly. 'I know just the thing,' said the witch with the crookedest fingers.

With that, the three witches huddled together, muttered some complicated words under their smelly breath and performed some hocus pocus as their bulging eyes luminesced. Donkey then disappeared into a cloud of thick smoke. Moments later, he reappeared coughing and spluttering. 'I can't see' gasped Donkey, fumbling about with his front hooves and tapping the ground haphazardly until the smoke cleared from his eyes. As he blinked, Donkey noticed something bothersome and shadowy hovering in his field of view. He shook his head sideways to try and get rid of it, but Donkey could still see it!

The three witches stood back and glared at donkey proudly. Their eyes continued to luminesce until the dregs of their spell finally dissipated. 'A fitting reward for the donkey who saved our lives,' said one of the witches, gesticulating with their wand. You have been honoured with the most distinguished gift ever awarded to an equine.

'Err, what's that ?' enquired Donkey nervously. One of the witches held up a mirror they had magicked out of thin air for Donkey to see. 'Arggh....' Donkey exclaimed in shock and surprise, as he saw himself in the mirror and jumped backwards. Donkey couldn't help but notice a long shiny horn sticking out of his forehead. 'Until now,' spouted the witch proudly, 'only a silver horn has ever been awarded. That was to a different equine, but your achievement was so great, that we've decided to give you a golden one.'

'Well...' said Donkey hesitantly, looking for the right words... 'I am sure I will get used to it.' He replied with mild anxiety in his voice. 'In fact, definitely' continued Donkey with certain gratitude, when he noticed the expectant look on the witches faces. He then admired his new horn in the mirror and quickly adapted to its presence. The witches were proud of their gift to Donkey and forged another blackened-tooth grimace. 'I think it complements your distinctive long ears,' said one of the witches, as she moved the mirror from left to right for Donkey to get a proper look.

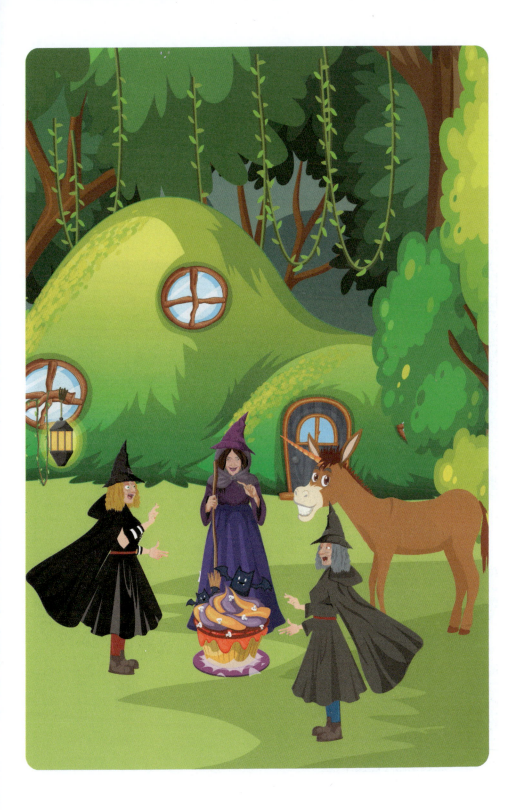

The spell cast on Donkey meant that he was frozen in time to live a long and happy life at the sanctuary where he is admired by all the other donkeys. He would give up his horn in a second though, if it was a choice between that or his donkey friends who mean more to him than anything.

We must also keep in mind that each and every donkey at the sanctuary is unique and special and each with their own story.

The witches magicked themselves back to their cavern where they celebrated the occasion in style with bat bunting, green cake decorated with eyeballs and invited all the spooks and ghouls from the neighbourhood to join them.

Meanwhile, the council assembled some solid barriers around the bottomless black hole without stairs, This would secure it until they could think of a more permanent solution to the danger it posed.

For the first time in history, a spell was cast to immortalize the noble donkey.

Frozen in time, Donkey continues to reside at the Animal Sanctuary today, refining the music of his bray and inspiring imagination and magic in others.

PS Don't be disappointed if you visit the sanctuary but don't manage to catch a glimpse of Donkey with his impressive horn. Now that he has magical properties, Donkey sometimes makes his horn invisible to people. This way, he can share all the attention from visitors with his donkey friends without being singled out for too much fuss. You could try and guess which one he might be ! Otherwise, he might be idling in the barn or shop, having some 'frozen time' for visitors to admire him. (Donkey might even shrink himself if he is somewhere short of space !) He may also be on tour, trying to help other donkeys in the country or simply taking a quiet nap somewhere, dreaming about his next carrot or mint treat from the staff !

PPS Don't forget to brush your teeth morning and night for a shiny smile instead of a gruesome grimace.

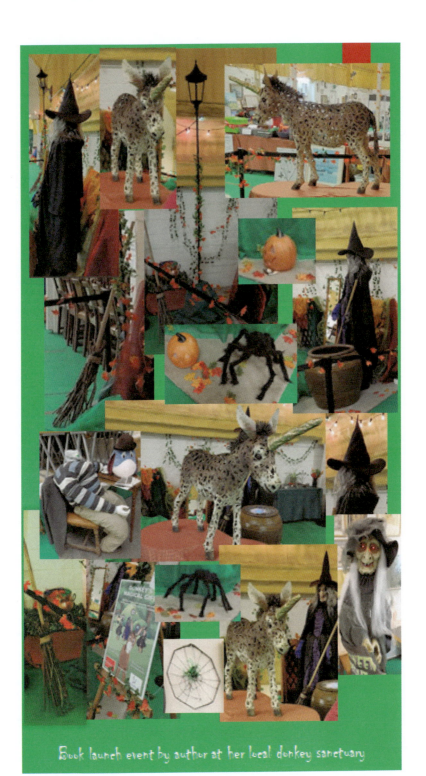

Book launch event by author at her local donkey sanctuary

Printed in Great Britain
by Amazon